WELCOME TO
PASSPORT TO READING
A beginning reader's ticket to a brand-new world!

Every book in this program is designed to build read-along and read-alone skills, level by level, through engaging and enriching stories. As the reader turns each page, he or she will become more confident with new vocabulary, sight words, and comprehension.

These PASSPORT TO READING levels will help you choose the perfect book for every reader.

READING TOGETHER
Read short words in simple sentence structures together to begin a reader's journey.

READING OUT LOUD
Encourage developing readers to sound out words in more complex stories with simple vocabulary.

READING INDEPENDENTLY
Newly independent readers gain confidence reading more complex sentences with higher word counts.

READY TO READ MORE
Readers prepare for chapter books with fewer illustrations and longer paragraphs.

This book features sight words from the educator-supported Dolch Sight Words List. This encourages the reader to recognize commonly used vocabulary words, increasing reading speed and fluency.

For more information, please visit passporttoreadingbooks.com.

Enjoy the journey!

Little, Brown and Company

Hachette Book Group
1290 Avenue of the Americas, New York, NY 10104
Visit our website at lb-kids.com

Little, Brown and Company is a division of Hachette Book Group, Inc.
The Little, Brown name and logo are trademarks of Hachette Book Group, Inc.

The publisher is not responsible for websites (or their content)
that are not owned by the publisher.

First Edition: July 2016

Library of Congress Control Number: 2016938206

ISBN 978-0-316-36146-0

10 9 8 7 6 5 4 3 2 1

CW

Printed in the United States of America

Passport to Reading titles are leveled by independent reviewers applying the standards developed by Irene Fountas and Gay Su Pinnell in *Matching Books to Readers: Using Leveled Books in Guided Reading*, Heinemann, 1999.

MEET KUBO

Adapted by R.R. Busse

Screenplay by Marc Haimes and Chris Butler

Story by Shannon Tindle and Marc Haimes

LITTLE, BROWN AND COMPANY
New York   Boston

Pay attention, Kubo fans!
Look for these words when you read this book.
Can you spot them all?

origami

helmet

bow

skeleton

This is Kubo.

He is a very brave boy.

He lives with his mother
in a hidden cave.

Kubo's mother stays in the cave.
She worries about Kubo a lot.

Kubo takes care of them both.

He makes money with his origami!

Origami is folding paper into shapes.

Kubo has an amazing power!

His origami comes
to life!

Little Hanzo is one of Kubo's origami creations.

He can point Kubo in the right direction with his magic.

One day, the Two Sisters
attack Kubo's home!
They are both great fighters
and very scary.

Kubo escapes!

Kubo must find three parts
of magical armor!
One is a breastplate, one is a
helmet, and one is a sword.

He needs all three pieces to
defeat the Two Sisters.

Soon, Kubo finds Monkey.
She helps Kubo and
keeps him safe.
Monkey is very serious.

Then Monkey and Kubo meet Beetle.

He is a big warrior.

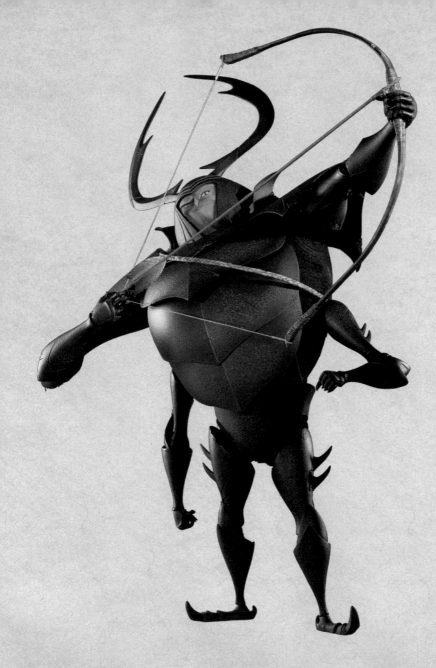

He and Monkey argue,
but he protects Kubo, too.
He uses a bow and arrows!

Kubo, Monkey, and Beetle
travel all over.
They must find the magical armor.

The Two Sisters
try to stop them!

23

Monsters are guarding each
piece of the armor.

This is the giant skeleton!

He has a lot of fake swords.

Kubo needs to find the right one!

Beware the Garden of Eyes!
It is deep underwater
and tries to eat Kubo!

The Two Sisters attack.

Monkey must rescue Kubo.

After that, they must fight

the evil Moon King!

He will do anything to stop Kubo!

Kubo has a long quest ahead of him.

His friends will help!

They get to know one another.

Kubo likes his new friends.

Kubo has all of the pieces
of armor he needs!
He is ready for his battle
with the Moon King.